Gilda
the Witch

by Terry Dinning

Illustrated by Angela Mills

Brimax • Newmarket • England

It is morning in the forest. Gilda the witch turns over in bed. "Time for another little snooze," she says sleepily. Gilda takes care of the forest with her magic spells. Her cottage is full of magical things. She has a broomstick, a cauldron, a crystal ball and shelves full of books. She also has a cat called Timothy.

Timothy leaps up onto Gilda's bed and licks the end of her nose.

"What is the matter, Timothy?" mumbles Gilda. "Why are you waking me up?" She sits up, and the tip of her witches' hat falls down over one eye. "What is that noise?" she wonders. She hears something odd over by the window.

Gilda leaps out of bed. Through the window she can see Katie and Bobby Rabbit scampering away in the distance, their white tails disappearing over the fields. The sky is blue, the grass is green and the daisies are white and yellow.

"How lovely!" sighs Gilda. "Today my spells will sweeten the bees' honey and make the roses smell like perfume."

Gilda is stirring her cauldron when there is a knock at the door. There stands Sally Squirrel. "Have you seen what has happened to the forest?" she squeaks. Gilda hurries outside. The trees are as tall as ever. The flowers smell as sweet as ever. Then Gilda sees what is wrong. The sky is not blue. It is green! The grass is not green. It is blue!

"One minute the sky was blue, and then it was green," says Sally. "You must cast a spell to make everything right again." "I need my magic spell book," says Gilda. She hunts along the bookshelves. She hunts under the table. She hunts among the cushions. "Where did I put that spell book?"

Timothy jumps onto the window-sill. He gives a loud meeow.

"Are you trying to tell me something?" asks Gilda. Suddenly she remembers what happened that morning, when she heard someone laughing outside the window. Gilda stares at the blue grass and the violet daisies. There are tiny footprints on the grass. "Those look like rabbits' footprints!" she says to herself.

"I know what has happened," Gilda tells Sally. "Someone has taken my spell book and I think I know who. Have you seen Bobby and Katie Rabbit this morning?"
"No," says Sally.
"When we find Bobby and Katie, I think we will find the spell book," says Gilda. "Then we can put everything right again. Come and help me look."

Gilda, Sally and Timothy set out on the trail of the missing spell book. Gilda flies along on her broomstick. Sally jumps from tree to tree. Timothy marches along with his whiskers in the air. They ask everyone they meet if they have seen Bobby and Katie.

"No," says Emma Duckling.
"No," says Hetty Hare.
"No," says Rosie Rabbit.

"No," says George Bear, busy in his garden, when Gilda tells him what has happened.
"I hope you find your book soon. I cannot tell my plums from my peaches until everything is put right again." Then Timothy begins to sniff at the bushes. He can hear something. He meeows again. Gilda can hear something too. It sounds just like two little rabbits crying.

''Is that you, Katie and Bobby?''
calls Gilda. Katie and Bobby
creep out from the bushes.
Bobby is carrying Gilda's
spell book.
''You naughty little rabbits,''
scolds Gilda. ''It was very wrong
to take my book without asking.''
''We are so sorry,'' sniffs Katie.
''We only wanted to borrow the
book, but we did not want to
wake you.''

"We wanted to make some magic spells," says Bobby. "We must have mixed them up, because when we said the magic words the sky turned green. And look!" Katie and Bobby turn around. Their tiny tails are not white, but blue!

"Never mind, you can help stir the cauldron while I say the spell that will change everything back to normal again."

Everyone goes home to Gilda's cottage. They wait while she finds all the magic things she needs. She needs early morning dew, some moonlight from a silver bottle, some cobwebs, and two hairs from a rabbit's tail.

"It does not matter if they are blue," she says. Then she reads out the spell from her spell book. "Abracadabra!" she cries.

They rush to the window. Gilda's spell has worked! The sky is blue. The grass is green.

"Well done," says Sally. "You are a good witch, Gilda." But Katie and Bobby still have their blue tails.

"They will be white again in a few days," Gilda says to them, "That will teach you not to meddle with magic!"

Say these words again.

forest	right
snooze	cushions
magic	laughing
cottage	whiskers
window	suddenly
distance	borrow
sweeten	meddle